Five Little Bats Flying in the Night

To my Lunch-bunch, Book Club buddies—S.M.

For Lynn and Bob—L.B.

ISBN 0-439-67259-7

12 11 10 9 8 7 6 5 4 3 2 1   5 6 7 8 9/0

Printed in the U.S.A.
First printing, September 2004

Five Little Bats Flying in the Night

by Steve Metzger
Illustrated by Laura Bryant

SCHOLASTIC INC.
New York   Toronto   London   Auckland   Sydney
Mexico City   New Delhi   Hong Kong   Buenos Aires

Five little bats flying in the night

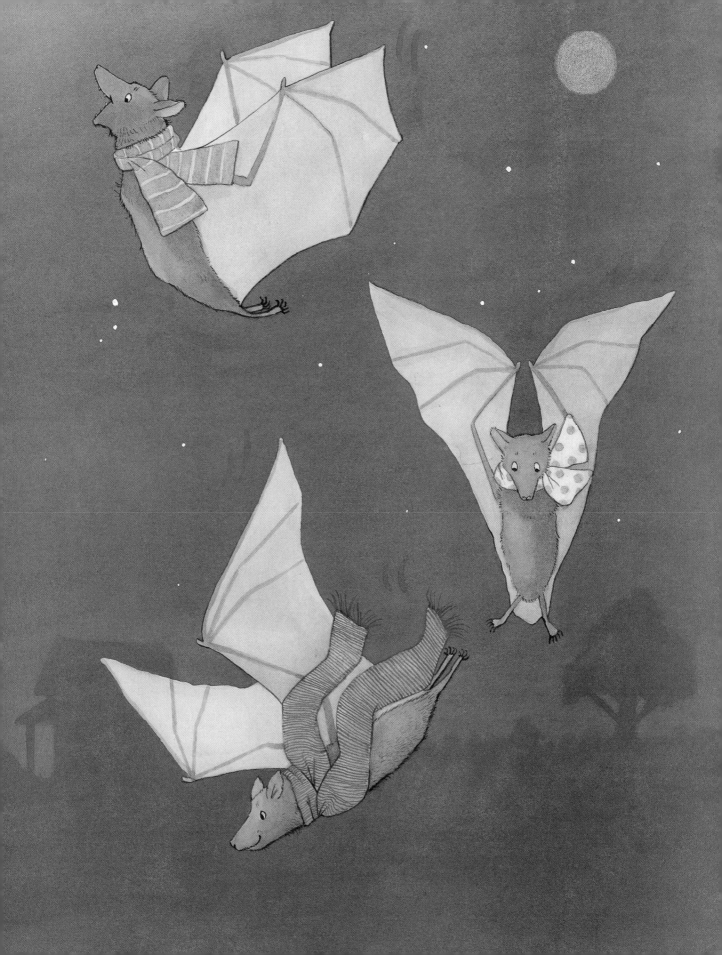

One flew away, far out of sight.

The mother called the doctor
and the doctor said,

"No more bats flying in the night!"

Four little bats flying all around.

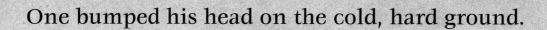
One bumped his head on the cold, hard ground.

The mother called the doctor and the doctor said,

"No more bats flying all around!"

Three little bats hanging upside down.

One fell off and began to frown.

The mother called the doctor and the doctor said,

"No more bats hanging upside down!"

Two little bats nibbling on a peach.

One got mad and began to screech.

The mother called the doctor and the doctor said,

"No more bats nibbling on a peach!"

One little bat flying near a lake…

...flew so close to a hungry snake.

The mother called the doctor and the doctor said,

"No more bats flying near a lake!"

Now there's...
No little bats flying in the sky.
No little bats flying way up high.

The mother called the doctor and the doctor said,